. . . *And the Earth Did Not Devour Him*

THE EXCHANGE

Does everyone have the same chance for success?

. . . *And the Earth*
Did Not Devour Him

Tomás Rivera

Translated by
Evangelina Vigil-Piñón

 HAMPTON-BROWN

. . . *And the Earth Did Not Devour Him* by Tomás Rivera. Copyright © 1987 by Concepción Rivera.
Copyright of translation © 1987 by Evangelina Vigil-Piñón. Cover design by Susan Barber.
Cover photograph by Carlos Rene Pérez. This edition is reprinted with permission from
Arte Público Press, University of Houston.

On-Page Coach™ (introductions, questions, on-page glossaries), The Exchange,
back cover summary © Hampton-Brown.

Hampton-Brown
P.O. Box 223220
Carmel, California 93922
800-333-3510
www.hampton-brown.com

Printed in the United States of America

ISBN-13: 978-0-7362-3181-7
ISBN-10: 0-7362-3181-1

06 07 08 09 10 11 12 13 14 15 10 9 8 7 6 5 4 3 2 1

Contents

Introduction

Tomás Rivera's novel . . . *And the Earth Did Not Devour Him* is considered a classic in Chicano, or Mexican American, literature. Like other Chicano literature published before the 1970s, this novel is about the social issues of Chicano people. Rivera's family emigrated from Mexico to Texas looking for work when Rivera was a boy. While Rivera uses real memories and experiences of being a migrant worker, this is a work of fiction.

. . . *And the Earth Did Not Devour Him* takes place during the late 1940s and early 1950s. During this time many Mexicans came to the United States to work. A lot of American men had left their jobs to fight in World War II. As a result, there were not enough workers in the U.S. In 1942, the U.S. and Mexican governments met to create a program under which Mexicans could come to the U.S. as temporary workers. This was called the Bracero Program.

The program was a mixed blessing for the Mexican workers. While it provided them with jobs, they were often treated unfairly. Rivera saw firsthand how migrant workers were **exploited** . He saw their suffering, but he

Key Concepts

exploit *v.* to unfairly use someone to benefit yourself

also saw their strength and **compassion** as they supported each other. He wanted to document and celebrate their lives. Following the style of contemporary Mexican and Latin American novelists, Rivera used a **fragmented** structure in this novel.

. . . *And the Earth Did Not Devour Him* is not a straight narrative, but a combination of chapters, **anecdotes**, thoughts, and conversations. While the book has this fragmented structure, there are elements that tie the stories together. The novel begins and ends with the story of a young boy's struggle to remember and understand a year in his life. Several of the chapters and anecdotes are

The Bracero Program

Between 1942 and 1964, more than four million Mexicans entered the U.S. under the Bracero Program. The *braceros,* or migrant workers, harvested crops and were sent back to Mexico when the harvesting season was over.

A lot of migrant workers were mistreated. They were physically abused and had money deducted from their wages. Most workers lived in shacks. Children frequently worked alongside their parents. They did not attend school. They grew weak from lack of nutrition and proper health care.

Key Concepts

compassion *n.* awareness of the suffering of another person and wanting to help them

fragmented *adj.* broken into parts; disconnected

anecdote *n.* short account of an incident

from the viewpoint of this young boy. The voices of other members of his community are heard as well.

Another element that ties the novel together is the anecdotes that introduce each chapter. These set the mood or introduce the story that follows. For example, on page 17, there is an anecdote about a visit by several mothers to a fortune-teller to find out what has happened to their sons. This anecdote introduces the following chapter called "A Prayer" in which a mother asks for protection for her son who is fighting in the war.

The structure of *. . . And The Earth Did Not Devour Him* seeks to imitate the way in which memory works. There are periods of confusion and feelings of being lost. These mimic feelings that the migrant workers might have had as they struggled to survive in the U.S. Together, all the different parts of the novel depict a community's struggle.

While Rivera struggled growing up as a migrant worker, he was able to graduate not only from high school but then he earned two college degrees. In 1979, he became chancellor at the University of California in Riverside. He remained there until his death in 1984. Rivera's life and published literature are inspirational. They are proof of just how far **determination** can take a person.

Key Concepts

determination *n.* strong intention and purpose to accomplish something

The Lost Year

That year was lost to him. At times he tried to remember and, just about when he thought **everything was clearing up some, he would be at a loss for words**. It almost always began with a dream in which he would suddenly awaken and then realize that he was really asleep. Then he wouldn't know whether what he was thinking had happened or not.

It always began when he would hear someone calling him by his name but when he turned his head to see who was calling, he would make a complete turn and there he would end up—in the same place. This was why he never could discover who was calling him nor why. And then he even forgot the name he had been called.

One time he stopped **at mid-turn and fear suddenly set in**. He realized that he had called himself. And thus the lost year began.

He tried to figure out when that time he had come to call "year" had started. He became aware that he was always thinking and thinking and from this there was no way out.

....

everything was clearing up some, he would be at a loss for words he understood everything, he suddenly did not know what to say or think

at mid-turn and fear suddenly set in in the middle of turning around and he became afraid suddenly

Then he started thinking about how he never thought and this was when **his mind would go blank** and he would fall asleep. But before falling asleep he saw and heard many things . . .

....

his mind would go blank he could not think anymore

What his mother never knew was that every night he would drink the glass of water that she left under the bed for the spirits. She always believed that they drank the water and so she continued **doing her duty**. Once he was going to tell her but then he thought that he'd wait and tell her when he was grown up.

....

doing her duty this religious custom; putting the glass of water under the bed

The Children Couldn't Wait

The heat had set in **with severity**. This was unusual because it was only the beginning of April and this kind of heat was not expected until the end of the month. It was so hot that the bucket of water the boss brought them was not enough. He would come only two times **for the midday and sometimes they couldn't hold out**. That was why they took to drinking water from a tank at the edge of the furrow. The boss had it there for the cattle and when he caught them drinking water there he got angry. He didn't much like the idea of their losing time going to drink water because they weren't on contract, but by the hour. He told them that if he caught them there again he was going to fire them and not pay them. The children were the ones who couldn't wait.

"I'm very thirsty, Dad. Is the boss gonna be here soon?"

"I think so. You can't wait any longer?"

"Well, I don't know. My throat already feels real dry. Do you think he's almost gonna be here? Should I go to the tank?"

....

with severity and it was extremely hot

for the midday and sometimes they couldn't hold out in the afternoon and sometimes they could not wait for him to bring them drinking water

"No, wait just a little longer. You already heard what he said."

"I know, that he'll fire us if he catches us there, but I can't wait."

"Come on now, come on, work. He'll be here real soon."

"Well . . . I'll try to wait. Why doesn't this one let us bring water? Up north . . ."

"Because he's **no good**, that's why."

"But we could hide it under the seat, couldn't we? It was always better up north . . . And what if I make like I'm gonna **go relieve myself** by the tank?"

And this was what they started doing that afternoon. They pretended they were going to relieve themselves and they would go on to the edge of the tank. The boss became aware of this almost right away. But he **didn't let on**. He wanted to catch a bunch of them and that way he could pay fewer of them and only after they had done more work. He noticed that one of the children kept going to drink water every little while and he became more and more furious. He thought then of giving him a scare and he crawled on the ground to get his rifle.

....

no good not a nice person
go relieve myself go to the bathroom
didn't let on pretended he did not know

What he set out to do and what he did were two different things. He shot at him once to scare him but when he pulled the trigger he saw the boy with a hole in his head. And the child didn't even jump like a deer does. He just stayed in the water like a dirty rag and the water began to turn bloody . . .

"They say that the old man almost went crazy."

"You think so?"

"Yes, he's already lost the ranch. He **hit the bottle pretty hard**. And then after **they tried him and he got off free**, they say he jumped off a tree 'cause he wanted to kill himself."

"But he didn't kill himself, did he?"

"Well, no."

"Well, there you have it."

"Well, I'll tell you, **compadre**, I think he did go crazy. You've seen the likes of him nowadays. He looks like a beggar."

"Sure, but that's 'cause he doesn't have any more money."

"Well . . . that's true."

....

hit the bottle pretty hard started drinking a lot

they tried him and he got off free he went to court and was not found guilty for killing the boy

compadre friend (in Spanish)

She had fallen asleep right away and everyone, **very mindful of not crossing** their arms nor their legs nor their hands, watched her intensely. The spirit was already present in her body.

"Let's see, how may I help you this evening, brothers and sisters?"

"Well, you see, I haven't heard from my boy in two months. Yesterday a letter from the government arrived telling me that he's **lost in action**. I'd like to know whether or not he's alive. I feel like I'm **losing my mind** just thinking and thinking about it."

"Have no fear, sister. Julianito is fine. He's just fine. Don't worry about him anymore. Very soon he'll be in your arms. He'll be returning already next month."

"Thank you, thank you."

....

very mindful of not crossing being very careful not to fold
lost in action missing in the war
losing my mind becoming crazy

A Prayer

Dear God, Jesus Christ, keeper of my soul. This is the third Sunday that I come to **implore** you, beg you, to **give me word of** my son. I have not heard from him. Protect him, my God, that no bullet may pierce his heart like it happened to Doña Virginia's son, may he rest in God's peace. Take care of him for me, Dear Jesus, save him from the gunfire, have pity on him who is so good. Since he was a baby, when I would nurse him to sleep, he was so gentle, very grateful, never biting me. He's very innocent, protect him, he does not wish to harm anyone, he is very noble, he is very kind, may no bullet **pierce his heart**.

Please, Virgin Mary, you, too, shelter him. Shield his body, cover his head, cover the eyes of the Communists and the Koreans and the Chinese so that they cannot see him, so they won't kill him. I still keep his toys from when he was a child, his little cars, little trucks, even a kite that I found the other day in the closet. Also his cards and the funnies that he has learned to read. I have put everything away until his return.

....

implore ask
give me word of tell me what has happened to
pierce his heart kill him

Protect him, Jesus, that they may not kill him. I have made a promise to the Virgen de San Juan to **pay her homage at her shrine** and to the Virgen de Guadalupe, too. He also wears a little medallion of the Virgen de San Juan del Valle and he, too, has made a promise to her; he wants to live. Take care of him, cover his heart with your hand, that no bullet may enter it. He's very noble. He was very afraid to go, he told me so. The day they took him, when he said his farewell he embraced me and he cried for a while. I could feel his heart beating and I remembered when he was little and I would nurse him and the happiness that I felt and he felt.

Take care of him for me, please, I **beseech** you. I promise you my life for his. Bring him back from Korea safe and sound. Cover his heart with your hands. Jesus Christ, Holy God, Virgen de Guadalupe, bring him back alive, bring me back his heart. Why have they taken him? He has done no harm. He knows nothing. He is very humble. He doesn't want to take away anybody's life. Bring him back alive, I don't want him to die.

Here is my heart for his. Here is my heart. Here, in my chest, **palpitating**. Tear it out if blood is what you want, but

....

pay her homage at her shrine honor her at her temple; show
her respect
beseech beg
palpitating beating hard

tear it out of *me*. I sacrifice my heart for his. Here it is. Here is my heart! Through it runs his very own blood . . .

Bring him back alive and I will give you my very own heart.

BEFORE YOU MOVE ON...

1. **Character** Describe the feelings of the boy in "The Lost Year." What is he trying to remember?

2. **Author's Style** How does the last line on page 12 help introduce the content that follows?

LOOK AHEAD Read to page 31 to see why the boy is forced to leave school.

"**Comadre**, do you all plan to go to Utah?"

"No, compadre. I'll tell you, we don't trust the man that's **contracting** people to go work in—how do you say it?"

"Utah. Why, comadre?"

"Because we don't think **there's such a state**. You tell me, when've you ever heard of that place?"

"Well, there's so many states. And this is the first time that they've contracted for work in those parts."

"Yeah, but tell me, where is it?"

"Well, we've never been there but I hear it's somewhere close to Japan."

....

Comadre Close friend (in Spanish)
contracting hiring
there's such a state Utah exists

It's That It Hurts

It hurts a lot. That's why I hit him. And now what do I do? Maybe they didn't **expel me from** school. Maybe it **ain't so**, after all. Maybe it's not. *Sure it is!* It is so, they did expel me. And now what do I do?

I think it all started when I got so embarrassed and angry at the same time. I **dread getting** home. What am I going to tell Mother? And then when Dad gets home from the fields? They'll whip me for sure. But it's embarrassing and angering. It's always the same in these schools in the north. Everybody just stares at you up and down. And then they make fun of you and the teacher with her popsicle stick, poking your head for lice. It's embarrassing. And then when they **turn up their noses**. It makes you angry. I think it's better staying out here on the ranch, here in the quiet of this knoll, with its chicken coops, or out in the fields where you at least feel more free, more at ease.

"Come on, son, we're almost there."
"You gonna take me to the principal?"

....

expel me from force me to leave
ain't so is not true
dread getting do not want to go
turn up their noses act like they are better than you

"Of course not. Don't tell me you don't know how to speak English yet. Look, that's the entrance over there. Just ask if you don't know where to go. Don't be shy, ask someone. Don't be afraid."

"Why can't you go in with me?"

"Don't tell me you're scared. Look, that's probably the entrance there. Here comes someone. Now, you behave, you hear me?"

"But why don't you help me?"

"No. You'll do just fine, don't be afraid."

It's always the same. They take you to the nurse and the first thing she does is check you for lice. And, too, those ladies are to blame. On Sundays they sit out in front of the chicken coops picking lice from each other's heads. And the **gringos**, passing by in their cars, looking and pointing at them. Dad is right when he says that they look like **monkeys in the zoo**. But it's not all that bad.

"Mother, you won't believe it. They took me out of the room. I had just walked in, and they put me in with a nurse all dressed in white. And they made me

....

gringos white people
monkeys in the zoo animals in a cage

take off my clothes and they even examined my behind. But where they took the longest was on my head. I had washed it, right? Well, the nurse brought out a jar of, like vaseline, it smelled like worm-killer, do I still smell? And she smeared it all over my head. It itched. And then she started **parting my hair** with a pencil. After a while they let me go but I was so ashamed because I had to take off my pants, even my underwear, in front of the nurse."

But now what do I tell them? That they **threw me out of** school? But it wasn't all my fault. I didn't like that gringo, **right off**. This one didn't laugh at me. He'd just stare and when they put me in the corner apart from everyone he kept turning to look at me, and then he'd make a gesture with his finger. I was mad but mostly I felt embarrassed because I was sitting away from everyone where they could see me better. Then when it was my turn to read, I couldn't. I could hear myself. And I could hear that no words were coming out . . . This cemetery isn't scary at all. That's what I like best about the walk to school and back. The greenness! And everything so even. The roads all paved. It even looks

....

parting my hair looking for lice
threw me out of made me leave
right off immediately; as soon as I saw him

like where they play golf. Today I won't have time to run up the hills and slide down tumbling. Nor to lie down on the grass and try to hear all the sounds. Last time I counted to 26 . . . If I hurry maybe I can go to the dump with Doña Cuquita. She **heads out** about this time when the sun's not so hot.

"Careful, children. Just be careful and don't step where there's fire burning underneath. Wherever you see smoke coming out, there's coals underneath. I know what I'm telling you, I once got a bad burn and I still have the scar . . . Look, each of you get a long stick and just turn the trash over briskly. If the dump man comes to see what we're doing, tell him we came to throw away some stuff. He's a kind man, but he likes to keep those little books with nasty pictures that people sometimes throw away . . . watch out for the train as you cross that bridge. It ran over a man last year . . . caught him right in middle of the bridge and he wasn't able to make it to the other side . . . Did they **give you permission** to come with me? . . . Don't eat anything until after you've washed it."

....

heads out leaves
give you permission say it was OK for you

But if I go with her without permission they'll whip me even more. What am I going to tell them? Maybe they didn't expel me. *Sure, they did!* Maybe not. *Yeah, they did!* What am I going to tell them? But it wasn't all my fault. I couldn't wait anymore. While I was standing there in the restroom he's the one that started **picking on** me.

"Hey, Mex . . . I don't like Mexicans because they steal. You hear me?"
"Yes."
"I don't like Mexicans. You hear, Mex?"
"Yes."
"I don't like Mexicans because they steal. You hear me?"
"Yes."

I remember the first fight I had at school. I got real scared because everything happened so slow. There wasn't any reason, it's just that some of the older boys who already had mustaches and who were still in the second grade started pushing us against each other. And they kept it up until we started fighting, I think, 'cause we were **plain** scared. It was

....

picking on being mean to; fighting with
plain so

about a block from school, I remember, when they started pushing me towards Ramiro. Then we began to **scuffle** and hit at each other. Some ladies came out and **broke us up**. Since then I got to feeling bigger. But all it was, up until I fought, was plain fear.

This time it was different. He didn't warn me. I just felt a real hard blow on my ear and I heard something like when you put a **conch** to your ear at the beach. I don't remember anymore how or when I hit him but I know I did because someone told the principal that we were fighting in the restroom. Maybe they didn't throw me out? *Sure they did!* And then, I wonder who called the principal? And the janitor all scared and with his broom up in the air, ready to swat me if I tried to leave.

"The Mexican kid got into a fight and beat up a couple of our boys . . . No, not bad . . . but what do I do?"

". . ."

"No, I guess not, they could care less if I expel him . . . They need him in the fields."

". . ."

....

scuffle fight
broke us up stopped us
conch large seashell

"Well, I just hope our boys don't make too much out about it to their parents. I guess I'll just throw him out."

". . ."

"Yeah, I guess you're right."

". . ."

"I know you warned me, I know, I know . . . but . . . yeah, ok."

But how could I even think of leaving knowing that everyone at home wanted me to go to school. Anyways, the janitor stood with his broom up in the air, **ready for anything** . . . And then they just told me to leave.

I'm halfway home. This cemetery is real pretty. It doesn't look anything like the one in Texas. That one *is* scary, I don't like it at all. What scares me the most is when we're leaving after a burial and I look up and I read the letters on the arch over the gate that say, *Don't forget me*. It's like I can hear all the dead people buried there saying these words and then the sound of these words stays in my mind and sometimes even if I don't look up when I pass through the gate, I still see them. But not this one, this one is real pretty. Just lots of soft grass and trees, I guess that's why here when

....

ready for anything prepared for me to fight back

people bury somebody they don't even cry. I like playing here. If only they would let us fish in the little creek that runs through here, there's lots of fish. But no, you even need **a license** to fish and then they don't even sell us one 'cause we're from out of state.

I won't be able to go to school anymore. What am I going to tell them? They've told me over and over that our teachers are like our second parents . . . and now? And when we get back to Texas everyone will find out, too. Mother and Dad will be angry; I might get more than just a whipping. And then my Uncle will find out and Grandpa. Maybe they might even send me to a **reform school** like the ones I've heard them talk about. There they turn you into a good person if you're bad. They're **real hard on you**. They leave you soft as a glove. But maybe they didn't expel me, *sure they did,* maybe not, *sure they did.* I could make like I'm going to school and stay here in the cemetery. That would be better. But then what? I could tell them that I lost my report card. And then what if I stay in the same grade? What hurt me the most is that now I won't be able to be a telephone operator like Dad wants me to. You need to finish school for that.

....

a license permission; a special permit
reform school school for teenagers with problems
real hard on you very strict

"Vieja, call m'ijo out here . . . look, compadre, ask your godson what he wants to be when he grows up and finishes school."

"What will you be, godson?"

"I don't know."

"Tell him! Don't be embarrassed. He's your godfather."

"What will you be, son?"

"A telephone operator."

"Is that so?"

"Yes, compadre, he's very determined, you know that? Every time we ask him he says he wants to be an operator. I think they pay well. I told the boss the other day and he laughed. I don't think he believes that my son can do it, but that's 'cause he doesn't know him. He's smarter than anything. I just pray God helps him finish school so he can become an operator."

That movie was good. The operator was the most important one. Ever since then I suppose that's why Dad has wanted me to study for that after I finish school. But . . . maybe they didn't throw me out. What if it's not true?

....

Vieja, call m'ijo out here Old woman, tell my godson to come here

Maybe not. *Sure, it is.* What do I tell them? What do I do? Now they won't be able to ask me what I'm going to be when I grow up. Maybe not. *No, yeah.* What do I do? It's that it hurts and it's embarrassing at the same time. I better just stay here. No, but then Mother will get scared like she does when there's lightning and thunder. I've gotta tell them. And when my **padrino** comes to visit us I'll just hide. **No need for him to find out.** Nor for me to read to him like Dad has me do every time he comes to visit us. What I'll do when he comes is hide behind the chest or under the bed. That way Dad and Mother won't feel embarrassed. And what if I really wasn't expelled? Maybe I wasn't? *No, yeah.*

....

padrino godfather (in Spanish)

No need for him to find out. It is not necessary for him to know.

> **BEFORE YOU MOVE ON...**
>
> 1. **Conclusions** Reread page 27. The school does not worry about expelling the narrator from school. Why?
>
> 2. **Character's Point of View** Why is the boy frightened to tell his parents that he cannot go to school anymore?
>
> **LOOK AHEAD** Read to page 48 to see what happens when the boy lives with terrible people.

"Why do **y'all** go to school so much?"

"My Dad says it's to prepare us. He says that if someday there's an opportunity, maybe they'll give it to us."

"Sure! If I were you I wouldn't worry about that. The poor can't get poorer. We can't get **worst off** than we already are. That's why I don't worry. The ones who have to **be on their toes** are the ones who are higher up. They've got something to lose. They can end up where we're at. But for us what does it matter?"

....

y'all all of you
worst off in a worse situation
be on their toes work hard; worry

Hand in His Pocket

Remember Don Laíto and Doña Bone? That's what everyone called them but their names were Don Hilario and Doña Bonifacia. Don't you remember? Well, I had to live with them for three weeks until school ended. At first I liked it but then later on I didn't.

Everything that people used to say about them **behind their backs** was true. About how they baked the bread, the pastries, how they would sometimes steal and that they **were bootleggers**. I saw it all. Anyways, they were good people but by the time school was about to end I was afraid of being with them in **that Model-T** that they had and even of sleeping in their house. And towards the end I didn't even feel like eating. That's why I'd go to the little neighborhood store to buy me some candy. And that's how I got along until my Dad, my Mother, and my brothers and sisters came to get me.

I remember they were very nice to me on the first day. Don Laíto laughed a lot and you could see his gold teeth and the rotten ones, too. And every little while Doña Bone,

....

behind their backs when they were not around

were bootleggers would sell the things they had stolen to other people

that Model-T their car

33

fat as could be, would grab me and squeeze me against her and I could feel her, real fat. They fed me dinner—I say *fed* me because *they* didn't eat. Now that I'm remembering, you know, I never saw them eat. The meat that she fried for me was green and it smelled really bad when she was cooking it. But after a while it didn't smell as much. But I don't know whether this was because I got used to the smell or because Don Laíto opened the window. Just parts of it tasted bad. I ate it all because I didn't want **to hurt their feelings**. Everybody liked Don Laíto and Doña Bone. Even **the Anglos** were fond of them. They gave them canned foods, clothes, toys. And when Don Laíto and Doña Bone weren't able to sell these to us, they'd give them to us. They would also pay us visits out in the fields to sell us Mexican sweetbread, thread and needles, canned food and nopalitos, and also shoes, coats and other things that sometimes were good, sometimes pretty bad.

"Won't you buy these shoes . . . oh, come on . . .
I know they're used, but they're the expensive kind
. . . look how they're not worn out yet . . . these . . .
I guarantee you, they last until they wear out . . ."

....

to hurt their feelings them to think that I did not like the food

the Anglos white people

34

I didn't want to seem ungrateful, so I ate it all. It made me sick. I had to spend a long time in the restroom. The worst of it was when I went to bed. They put me in a room with no light and that smelled musty and was crowded with things: boxes, bottles, **almanacs**, bundles of clothing. There was only one entrance. You couldn't even see the windows with so many things all piled up. The first night I hardly slept because I was sure that spiders would be crawling down from the hole in the ceiling. Everything smelled so awful. By the time it grew dark I couldn't see anything, but it must have been around midnight when I woke up. I think I had fallen asleep, but I'm not too sure. The only thing I could see was that real dark hole in the ceiling. It seemed I could see faces but it was just my imagination. In any case, **fear got the best of me**. And I wasn't able to sleep anymore. Only at dawn when I could see the rest of the things in the room. Sometimes I would imagine Don Laíto and Doña Bone seated around me and there were times when I would even reach my hand out to touch them, but there was nothing. I think that from that very first day I wanted them to come get me. Something in my heart told me that something would happen. It's not that they weren't good

....

almanacs reference books
fear got the best of me I became terrified

people, they were, but like they say, they had their bad side.

At school, classes were going well. Sometimes when I came back from school in the afternoon not a sound could be heard in the small house and it seemed like no one was around. But always, when I was feeling most at peace, Doña Bone would scare me. She'd grab me from behind and laugh, and me, I'd jump, I was so scared. And she would just laugh and laugh. The first few times I'd end up laughing, too, but later I got tired of it. Then later on they told me **bit by bit** what they would do when they went downtown. They stole lots of things: food, liquor, clothes, cigarettes, even meat. When they weren't able to sell it to the neighbors, they gave it away. They would get rid of almost everything. Another thing, after a few days they invited me to see how they made sweet bread. Don Laíto would take off his shirt. He looked very hairy. He would start sweating as he kneaded the dough. But it was when he would stick his hands under his arms and then keep on kneading the dough that made me the sickest. It was true what people said. He would look at me to see if I was getting **nauseous** and he would tell me that this was what all the bakers did. One thing for sure, I never again ate any of the sweet bread that he baked, even

....

bit by bit more information about
nauseous sick, disgusted

though they sometimes had a bunch of it on the table.

I remember one day after school they put me to work in the yard. Not that it was so hard, but since that moment they had me working all the time. They wanted me to work at all hours. It's that my Dad had paid them for **my board**! One time they even wanted me to try to steal a five-pound sack of flour. Can you imagine? I was scared, and besides, it wasn't right. Don Laíto would just laugh and tell me that I didn't have any balls. Anyway, the days went on this way until, sometimes, I even felt like leaving, but how could I? My Dad had left me there and he had spent his money. The food got worse, and it got to be all work all the time.

And then . . . I'll tell you something . . . but please don't tell anyone. I noticed that this **wetback** started coming to the house while Don Laíto was away. I don't know how he knew when he wasn't there. Anyway, if I happened to be inside the house, Doña Bone would **throw me out**, and if I wasn't inside she would latch the doors and I knew I wasn't supposed to enter. One time Doña Bone tried to explain the whole thing to me but, to be very honest, I felt embarrassed and I hardly heard anything she told me. I did know that he left her money. Whoever he was, he was old and every time

....

my board me to live there
wetback illegal immigrant (negative slang)
throw me out make me leave

he came he smelled of shaving lotion and the smell would **linger** for a good while after he left. One night I overheard a conversation between the old couple.

"This guy has money and, besides that, he doesn't have any relatives. Look, viejo, it would be so easy. Not even anyone to worry about him . . . I don't think so, do you? . . . That boss could care less, he darn sure knows that he's a wetback and if something happens to him, you think he'll be concerned about him? Nobody knows that he comes here . . . you just leave it up to me . . . Oh, that'll be so easy . . ."

The next day, after school, they **marked** a square on the ground in the yard under some trees, and they told me that they wanted to build a cellar and that they wanted me to start digging there, little by little. They were going to use it to store the jars of **preserves** that Doña Bone made. It took me three days to dig somewhat deep and then they told me to stop digging, that they weren't going to build it after all. And then came the **good part**.

I remember well that the wetback arrived, his hair

....

linger stay
marked drew
preserves jam, jelly
good part part that you cannot tell anyone about

combed real good and fragrant, like always. At dusk Doña Bone called me to come eat. There was Don Laíto, already, but I didn't know how he had entered. After dinner they told me to go to bed right away.

I **got the scare of my life** when I stretched out on the bed and I touched what felt like a snake but what was in reality the wetback's arm. I thought he must be drunk because he didn't wake up. I jumped back and got out of the room. The old couple **burst into laughter**. Then I noticed that part of my shirt was full of blood. I didn't know what to think. I just remember Don Laíto's gold teeth and his rotten ones.

When it got real dark they made me help them drag him out and throw him into the hole that I myself had dug. As for me, I didn't really want to but then they told me that they would tell the police that I had killed him. I thought of how my Dad had paid them for my room and board and how even the Anglos liked them so much. All that my parents wanted was for me to finish school so I could find me some job that wasn't so hard. I was real scared but I went ahead and threw him in the hole. Then the three of us threw dirt over him. I never saw his face. All I wanted

....

got the scare of my life was shocked; was terrified
burst into laughter started laughing

was for school to end so they would come for me. The two weeks left went by very slowly. I thought that I'd get over my **fright** or that I'd be able to forget about it, but no. Don Laíto was even wearing the wetback's wrist watch. In the yard you could see **the mound of dirt**.

When my Dad and my Mother finally came for me they told me that I was very thin and that I looked like I was sick from fright. I told them no, that it was because I played so much at school and after school. Before we left, Don Laíto and Doña Bone squeezed me and told me in loud voices, so that Dad could hear, not to say anything or they would tell the police. Then they started laughing and I noticed that Dad had taken it as a joke. On the way to the farm they talked about how kind Don Laíto and Doña Bone were and how everyone liked them so much. I just kept looking out the car window and telling them yes. After about two months or so, just about when it seemed that I was forgetting all about it, they came to visit us at the farm. They had a present for me. A ring. They made me put it on and I remembered that it was the one the wetback had on that day. As soon as they left I tried to throw it away but I don't know why I couldn't. I thought that someone might find it.

....

fright fear, shock
the mound of dirt where the man was buried

And the worst was that for a long time, as soon as I would see a stranger, I'd slip my hand into my pocket. **That habit stayed with me** for a long time.

....

That habit stayed with me I kept doing that

It was an hour before the afternoon movie started. He needed a haircut, so he went into the barber shop across the street from the theater. At first he didn't quite understand, so he sat down and waited. But then the barber told him again that he couldn't cut his hair. He thought the barber didn't have time, so he remained seated waiting for the other barber. When he was finished with the **client**, he got up and walked to the barber's chair. But this barber told him the same thing. That he couldn't cut his hair. Furthermore, he told him that it would be better if he left. He crossed the street and stood there waiting for the theater to open, but then the barber came out and told him to leave. Then **it all became clear to him** and he went home to get his father.

....

client other customer

it all became clear to him he began to understand why they would not cut his hair

A Silvery Night

It was a silvery night when he called the devil.
Everything was almost clear and it even smelled like day.
The whole day he thought about what could happen to
him, but the more he thought about it the more curious he
became and the less fearful. So that by the time everybody
went to bed and turned off the lights, he had already decided
to go out right at midnight. He would have to slide across
the floor to the door without anyone hearing or seeing him.

"Dad. Why don't you leave the door open. There
aren't any mosquitos, anyway."

"Yes, but what if some animal gets in. You remember
that badger that got into the Flores' home."

"But that was two years ago. Come on, leave it open.
It's real hot. Nothing's gonna get in. All that's left around
here are crows, and those don't get into people's houses.
Come on. See how all the other people leave their
doors open."

"Yes, but at least they've got screens."

....

It was a silvery night The night sky looked gray and silver

"Not all of them. Please. See how pretty the moon looks. Everything is so peaceful."

"All right . . . No, Vieja, no animal is going to crawl in. You and your fears."

The devil had fascinated him as far back as he could remember. Even when they had taken him to the shepherds plays at his Aunt Pana's, he was already curious about how it might look. He thought about Don Rayos, with his black metal mask, with his red horns and black cape. Then he remembered how he found the costume and the mask under Don Rayos' house. One of his marbles had rolled under the house and when he reached for it he found everything all full of dust. He pulled everything out, dusted it off and then he put on the mask.

"I tell you, compadre, you don't fool around with the devil. There are many who have **summoned him and have regretted it** afterwards. Most of them go insane. Sometimes they get together in groups to summon him, so they won't be afraid. But he doesn't appear before them until later, when each of them is alone, and he

....

The devil had fascinated him He had always been interested in the devil

summoned him and have regretted it asked for him and wished they had not

appears in different shapes. No, nobody should fool with the devil. If you do, as they say, you give up your soul. Some die of fright, others don't. They just start looking real **somber** and then they don't even talk anymore. It's like **their spirits have left their bodies**."

From where he was lying on the floor he could see the clock on the table. He sensed each of his brothers and sisters falling asleep, one by one, and then his parents. He thought he could even make out the sound of snores coming from the other chicken shacks. Eleven to eleven-fifty went by the slowest. Occasionally, he felt somewhat fearful, but then he would look outside where everything was so still and serene under the silvery light of the moon and his fears quickly passed.

"If I leave here at eleven-fifty I'll have enough time to get to the center of the **knoll**. Good thing there's no snakes here, otherwise it'd be dangerous walking through the weeds that grow so tall at the center of the knoll. I'll call him right at twelve. I better take the clock so I'll know when it's exactly twelve. Otherwise, he might not

....

somber sad, depressed

their spirits have left their bodies they are dead inside; they have no soul

knoll small hill

come. It has to be right at midnight, exactly midnight."

Very slowly, without making a sound, he left, picking up the clock from the table. He put it in his pants' pocket and he noticed that it ticked louder inside the pocket than outside. Even once he was past the chicken coops he walked very slowly, stepping carefully and stopping every now and then. He felt someone was watching him. He proceeded cautiously until he had passed the **outhouse**. From there the chicken coops were barely visible and he began talking to himself but very softly.

"And how do I call him? Maybe he'll appear. No, I don't think so. In any case, if he does appear he can't do anything to me. I haven't died yet. So he can't do anything to me. I'd just like to know whether there is or isn't . . . If there isn't a devil, maybe there also isn't . . . No, I better not say it. I might get punished. But if there's no devil maybe there's no punishment. No, there has to be punishment. Well, how do I call him? Just, devil? Or, imp? Or, demon? Lucifer? Satan? . . .

....

outhouse outdoor bathroom

Whatever comes first."

He got to the center of the knoll and summoned him. At first no words came out, from pure fright, but then his name slipped out in a loud voice and nothing happened. He kept calling him by different names. And nothing. No one came out. Everything looked the same. Everything was the same. All peaceful. Then he thought it would be better to curse the devil instead. So he did. He swore at him using all the **cuss** words that he knew and in different tones of voice. He even cursed the devil's mother. But nothing. Nothing nor no one appeared, nor did anything change. **Disillusioned** and feeling at moments a little brave, he headed back for the house. The sound of the wind rustling the leaves of the trees seemed to accompany his every step. There was no devil.

"But if there's no devil neither is there . . . No, I better not say it. I might get punished. But there's no devil. Maybe he'll appear before me later. No, he would've appeared already. What better time than at night and me, alone? No, there's no devil. There isn't."

....

cuss foul, bad
Disillusioned Feeling like there was no devil

Two or three different times he **sensed someone** calling him but he didn't want to turn around. He didn't get scared because he felt sure that it wasn't anyone nor anything. After he laid down, very careful not to make a sound, certain that there was no devil, he began to feel chills and his stomach became upset. Before falling asleep he thought for a good while. *There is no devil, there is nothing.* The only thing that had been present in the woods was his own voice. No wonder, he thought, people said you shouldn't fool around with the devil. Now he understood everything. Those who summoned the devil went crazy, not because the devil appeared, but just the opposite, because he didn't appear. He fell asleep gazing at the moon as it jumped through the clouds and the trees, as if it were extremely content about something.

....

sensed someone thought someone was

BEFORE YOU MOVE ON...

1. **Conclusions** Reread pages 40–41. Why does the boy put his hand into his pocket whenever he meets a stranger?

2. **Inference** Reread page 42. Why is the boy forced to leave the barbershop?

LOOK AHEAD Read pages 49–68 to find out why the boy thinks that he is buried alive.

One afternoon a minister from one of the protestant churches in the town came to the farm and informed them that some man would be coming to teach them **manual skills** so that they would no longer have to work just in the fields. Practically all of the men got excited. He was going to teach them **carpentry**. A man came about two weeks later in a station wagon hauling a trailer. He brought with him the minister's wife to **assist him as interpreter**. But they never taught them anything. They would spend the entire day inside the trailer. A week later they left without a word. They later learned that the man had run off with the minister's wife.

....

manual skills how to work with tools and machines

carpentry how to build things

assist him as interpreter help him communicate with Spanish speakers

And the Earth Did Not Devour Him

The first time he felt hate and anger was when he saw his mother crying for his uncle and his aunt. They both **had caught tuberculosis** and had been sent to different **sanitariums**. So, between the brothers and sisters, they had split up the children among themselves and had taken care of them as best they could. Then the aunt died, and soon thereafter they brought the uncle back from the sanitarium, but he was already spitting blood. That was when he saw his mother crying every little while. He became angry because he was unable to do anything against anyone. Today he felt the same. Only today it was for his father.

"You all should've come home right away, m'ijo. Couldn't you see that your Daddy was sick? You should have known that **he'd suffered a sunstroke**. Why didn't you come home?"

"I don't know. Us being so soaked with sweat, we didn't feel so hot, but I guess that when you're sunstruck it's different. But I did tell him to sit down under the tree

....

had caught tuberculosis had a terrible lung disease

sanitariums hospitals

he'd suffered a sunstroke he had become sick from staying in the sun too long

that's at the edge of the rows, but he didn't want to. And that was when he started throwing up. Then we saw he couldn't hoe anymore and we dragged him and put him under a tree. He didn't **put up a fuss** at that point. He just let us take him. He didn't even say a word."

"Poor viejo, my poor viejo. Last night he hardly slept. Didn't you hear him outside the house. He squirmed in bed all night with cramps. God willing, he'll get well. I've been giving him cool lemonade all day, but his eyes still look **glassy**. If I'd gone to the fields yesterday, I tell you, he wouldn't have gotten sick. My poor viejo, he's going to have cramps all over his body for three days and three nights at the least. Now, you all take care of yourselves. Don't overwork yourselves so much. Don't **pay any mind to** that boss if he tries to rush you. Just don't do it. He thinks it's so easy since he's not the one who's out there stooped."

He became even angrier when he heard his father moan outside the chicken coop. He wouldn't stay inside because he said it made him feel very anxious. Outside where he could feel the fresh air was where he got some relief. And also

....

put up a fuss argue with us
glassy lifeless, expressionless
pay any mind to listen to

when the cramps came he could roll over on the grass. Then he thought about whether his father might die from the sunstroke. At times he heard his father start to pray and ask for God's help. At first he had faith that he would get well soon but by the next day he felt the anger growing inside of him. And all the more when he heard his mother and his father **clamoring** for God's mercy. That night, well past midnight, he had been awakened by his father's groans. His mother got up and removed the **scapularies** from around his neck and washed them. Then she lit some candles. But nothing happened. It was like his aunt and uncle all over again.

"What's **to be gained** from doing all that, Mother? Don't tell me you think it helped my aunt and uncle any. How come we're like this, like we're **buried alive**? Either the germs eat us alive or the sun burns us up. Always some kind of sickness. And every day we work and work. For what? Poor Dad, always working so hard. I think he was born working. Like he says, barely five years old and already helping his father plant corn. All the time feeding the earth and the sun, only to one day,

....

clamoring praying
scapularies religious cloths
to be gained going to change
buried alive being eaten by the earth

just like that, get struck down by the sun. And there you are, helpless. And them, begging for God's help . . . why, God doesn't care about us . . . I don't think there even is . . . No, better not say it, what if Dad gets worse. Poor Dad, I guess that at least gives him some hope."

His mother noticed how furious he was, and that morning she told him to calm down, that everything was in God's hands and that with God's help his father was going to get well.

"Oh, Mother, do you really believe that? I am certain that God **has no concern for** us. Now you tell me, is Dad evil or mean-hearted? You tell me if he has ever done any harm to anyone."

"Of course not."

"So there you have it. You see? And my aunt and uncle? You explain. And the poor kids, now orphans, never having known their parents. Why did God have to take them away? I tell you, God could care less about the poor. Tell me, why must we live here like this? What have we done to deserve this? You're so good and yet

---

has no concern for does not care about

you have to suffer so much."

"Oh, please, m'ijo, don't talk that way. Don't speak against the will of God. Don't talk that way, please, m'ijo. You scare me. It's as if already the blood of Satan runs through your veins."

"Well, maybe. That way at least, I could get rid of this anger. I'm so tired of thinking about it. Why? Why you? Why Dad? Why my uncle? Why my aunt? Why their kids? Tell me, Mother, why? Why us, **burrowed** in the dirt like animals with no hope for anything? You know the only hope we have is **coming out here** every year. And like you yourself say, only death brings rest. I think that's the way my aunt and uncle felt and that's how Dad must feel, too."

"That's how it is, m'ijo. Only death brings us rest."

"But why us?"

"Well, they say that . . ."

"Don't say it. I know what you're going to tell me—that the poor go to heaven."

That day started out cloudy and he could feel the morning coolness brushing his eyelashes as he and his

....

burrowed buried, stuck
coming out here making money as migrant workers

brothers and sisters began the day's labor. Their mother had to stay home to care for her husband. Thus, he felt responsible for **hurrying on** his brothers and sisters. During the morning, at least for the first few hours, they endured the heat but by ten-thirty the sun had suddenly cleared the skies and **pressed down against the world**. They began working more slowly because of the weakness, dizziness, and suffocation they felt when they worked too fast. Then they had to wipe the sweat from their eyes every little while because their vision would get blurred.

"If you start **blacking out**, stop working, you hear me? Or go a little slower. When we reach the edge we'll rest a bit to get our strength back. It's gonna be hot today. If only it'd stay just a bit cloudy like this morning, then nobody would complain. But no, once the sun **bears down** like this not even one little cloud dares to appear out of fear. And the worst of it is we'll finish up here by two and then we have to go over to that other field that's nothing but hills. It's okay at the top of the hill but down in the lower part of the slopes it gets to be real suffocating. There's no breeze there. Hardly any air

....

hurrying on taking care of
pressed down against the world heated up the ground
blacking out to faint
bears down shines brightly

goes through. Remember?"

"Yeah."

"That's where the hottest part of the day will **catch us**. Just drink plenty of water every little while. It don't matter if the boss gets mad. Just don't get sick. And if you can't go on, tell me right away, all right? We'll go home. Y'all saw what happened to Dad when he pushed himself too hard. The sun has no mercy, it can eat you alive."

Just as they had **figured**, they had moved on to the other field by early afternoon. By three o'clock they were all soaked with sweat. Not one part of their clothing was dry. Every little while they would stop. At times they could barely breathe, then they would black out and they would become fearful of getting sunstruck, but they kept on working.

"How do y'all feel?"

"Man, it's so hot! But we've got to keep on. 'Til six, at least. Except this water don't help our thirst any. Sure wish I had a bottle of cool water, real cool, fresh from the well, or a coke ice-cold."

"Are you crazy? That'd sure make you sunsick right now. Just don't work so fast. Let's see if we can make it

....

catch us affect us

figured thought, guessed

until six. What do you think?"

At four o'clock the youngest became ill. He was only nine years old, but since he was paid the same as a grown up he tried to keep up with the rest. He began vomiting. He sat down, then he laid down. Terrified, the other children ran to where he lay and looked at him. It appeared that he had fainted and when they opened his eyelids they saw his eyes were rolled back. The next youngest child started crying but right away he told him to stop and help him carry his brother home. It seemed he was having cramps all over his little body. He lifted him and carried him by himself and, again, he began asking himself *why?*

"Why Dad and then my little brother? He's only nine years old. Why? He has to **work like a mule buried in the earth**. Dad, Mom, and my little brother here, what are they guilty of?"

Each step that he took towards the house **resounded with** the question, *why?* About halfway to the house he began to get furious. Then he started crying out of rage. His little

....

work like a mule buried in the earth work so hard that he gets sick

resounded with made him think of

brothers and sisters did not know what to do, and they, too, started crying, but out of fear. Then he started cursing. And without even realizing it, he said what he had been wanting to say for a long time. He cursed God. Upon doing this he felt that fear instilled in him by the years and by his parents. For a second he saw the earth opening up to **devour** him. Then he felt his footsteps against the earth, compact, more solid than ever. Then his anger swelled up again and he **vented it** by cursing God. He looked at his brother, he no longer looked sick. He didn't know whether his brothers and sisters had understood **the graveness of his curse**.

That night he did not fall asleep until very late. He felt at peace as never before. He felt as though he had become detached from everything. He no longer worried about his father nor his brother. All that he awaited was the new day, the freshness of the morning. By daybreak his father was doing better. He was on his way to recovery. And his little brother, too; the cramps had almost completely subsided. Frequently he felt a sense of surprise upon recalling what he had done the previous afternoon. He thought of telling his mother, but he decided to keep it secret. All he told her was that the earth did not devour anyone, nor did the sun.

....

devour destroy, swallow
vented it expressed it; let it out
the graveness of his curse how wrong it was to curse God

He left for work and **encountered** a very cool morning. There were clouds in the sky and for the first time he felt capable of doing and undoing anything that he pleased. He looked down at the earth and kicked it hard and said:

"Not yet, you can't swallow me up yet. Someday, yes. But **I'll never know it**."

....

encountered realized it was
I'll never know it not if I can stop it

A stroke left the grandfather **paralyzed** from the neck down. One day one of his grandsons came by to visit with him. The grandfather asked him how old he was and what he most desired in life. The grandson replied that what he most wanted was for the next ten years to pass by immediately so that he would know what had happened in his life. The grandfather told him he was very stupid and **cut off** the conversation. The grandson did not understand why he had called him stupid until he turned thirty.

....

paralyzed unable to move
cut off ended

First Communion

The priest always held First Communion during mid-spring. I'll always remember that day in my life. I remember what I was wearing and I remember my godfather and the pastries and chocolate that we had after mass, but I also remember what I saw at the cleaners that was next to the church. I think it all happened because I left so early for church. It's that I hadn't been able to sleep the night before, trying to remember all of my sins, and worse yet, trying to arrive at an exact number. Furthermore, since Mother had placed a picture of hell at the head of the bed and since the walls of the room were papered with images of the devil and since I wanted **salvation** from all evil, that was all I could think of.

"Remember, children, very quiet, very very quiet. You have learned your prayers well, and now you know which **are the mortal sins and which are the venial sins**, now you know what **sacrilege is**, now you know that you are God's children, but you can also be children of the devil. When you go to confession you must tell all

....

salvation to be forgiven and saved

are the mortal sins and which are the venial sins sins are worse than other sins

sacrilege is it is to disobey religious rules

of your sins, you must try to remember all of the sins you have committed. Because if you forget one and receive Holy Communion then that would be a sacrilege and if you commit sacrilege you will go to hell. God knows all. You cannot lie to God. You can lie to me and to the priest, but God knows everything; so if your soul is not **pure of** sin, then you should not receive Holy Communion. That would be a sacrilege. So everyone confess all of your sins. **Recall** all of your sins. Wouldn't you be ashamed if you received Holy Communion and then later remembered a sin that you had forgotten to confess? Now, let's see, let us practice confessing our sins. Who would like to start off? Let us begin with the sins that we commit with our hands when we touch our bodies. Who would like to start?"

The nun liked for us to talk about the sins of the flesh. The real truth was that we practiced a lot telling our sins, but the real truth was that I didn't understand a lot of things. What did scare me was the idea of going to hell because some months earlier I had fallen against a small basin filled with hot coals which we used as a heater in the little room

....

pure of empty of
Recall Remember

where we slept. I had burned my calf. I could well imagine how it might be to burn in hell forever. That was all that I understood. So I spent that night, the eve of my First Communion, going over all the sins I had committed. But what was real hard was coming up with the exact number like the nun wanted us to. It must have been dawn by the time I finally **satisfied my conscience**. I had committed one-hundred-and-fifty sins, but I was going to admit to two hundred.

"If I say one hundred and fifty, and I've forgotten some, that would be bad. I'll just say two hundred and that way even if I forget lots of them I won't commit any kind of sacrilege. Yes, I have committed two-hundred sins . . . Father, I have come to confess my sins . . . How many? . . . Two hundred . . . of all kinds . . . **The Commandments?** Against all of the Ten Commandments . . . This way there will be no sacrilege. It's better this way. By confessing more sins you'll be purer."

I remember I got up much earlier that morning than

....

satisfied my conscience counted all the sins I had committed and felt satisfied

The Commandments? The rules in the Bible?

Mother had expected. My godfather would be waiting for me at the church and I didn't want to be even one second late.

"Hurry, Mother, get my pants ready, I thought you already ironed them last night."

"It's just that I couldn't see anymore last night. My eyesight is failing me now and that's why I had to leave them for this morning. But tell me, what's your hurry now? It's still very early. Confession isn't until eight o'clock and it's only six. Your padrino won't be there until eight."

"I know, but I couldn't sleep. Hurry, Mother, I want to leave now."

"And what are you going to do there so early?"

"Well, I want to leave because I'm afraid I'll forget the sins I have to confess to the priest. I can think better at the church."

"All right, I'll be **through** in just a minute. Believe me, as long as I can see I'm able to do a lot."

I **headed for** church repeating my sins and **reciting the Holy Sacraments**. The morning was already bright and

....

through finished
headed for went to
reciting the Holy Sacraments praying out loud

clear but there weren't many people out in the street yet. The morning was cool. When I got to the church I found that it was closed. I think the priest might have **overslept** or was very busy. That was why I walked around the church and passed by the cleaners that was next to the church. The sound of loud laughter and moans surprised me because I didn't expect anybody to be in there. I thought it might be a dog but then it sounded like people again and that's why I peeked in through the little window in the door. They didn't see me but I saw them. They were naked and embracing each other, lying on some shirts and dresses on the floor. I don't know why but I couldn't move away from the window. Then they saw me and tried to cover themselves, and they yelled at me to get out of there. The woman's hair looked all messed up and she looked like she was sick. And me, to tell the truth, I got scared and ran to the church but I couldn't **get my mind off of** what I had seen. I realized then that maybe those were the sins that we committed with our hands. But I couldn't forget the sight of that woman and that man lying on the floor. When my friends started arriving I was going to tell them but then I thought it would be better to tell them after communion.

....

overslept slept late; not woken up on time
get my mind off of stop thinking about

More and more I was feeling like I was the one who had committed a sin of the flesh.

"There's nothing I can do now. But I can't tell the others 'cause they'll sin like me. I better not go to communion. Better that I don't go to confession. I can't, now that I know, I can't. But what will Mom and Dad say if I don't go to communion? And my padrino, I can't leave him there waiting. I have to confess what I saw. I feel like going back. Maybe they're still there on the floor. No choice, I'm gonna have to lie. What if I forget it between now and confession? Maybe I didn't see anything? And if I hadn't seen anything?"

I remember that when I went in to confess and the priest asked for my sins, all I told him was two hundred and of all kinds. I did not confess the sin of the flesh. On returning to the house with my godfather, everything seemed changed, like I was and yet wasn't in the same place. Everything seemed **smaller and less important**. When I saw my Dad and my Mother, I imagined them on the floor. I started seeing all of the grown-ups naked and their faces even

....

smaller and less important ordinary compared to what I had seen looked **distorted**, and I could even hear them laughing and moaning, even though they weren't even laughing. Then I started imagining the priest and the nun on the floor. I couldn't hardly eat any of the sweet bread or drink the chocolate. As soon as I finished, I recall running out of the house. It felt like I couldn't breathe.

"So, what's the matter with him? Such manners!"

"Ah, compadre, let him be. You don't have to be concerned on my account. I have my own. These young ones, all they can think about is playing. Let him have a good time, it's the day of his First Communion."

"Sure, compadre, I'm not saying they shouldn't play. But they have to learn to be more **courteous**. They have to show more respect toward adults, their elders, and all the more for their padrino."

"No, well, that's true."

I remember I headed toward the **thicket**. I picked up some rocks and threw them at the cactus. Then I broke some bottles. I climbed a tree and stayed there for a long time until I got tired of thinking. I kept remembering the scene

....

distorted strange, weird
courteous polite
thicket thick bushes

at the cleaners, and there, alone, I even liked recalling it. I even forgot that I had lied to the priest. And then I felt the same as I once had when I had heard a missionary speak about **the grace of God**. I felt like knowing more about everything. And then it occurred to me that maybe everything was the same.

....

the grace of God the love and protection of God

BEFORE YOU MOVE ON...

1. **Conflict** Reread pages 50–54. What causes the boy to feel like the earth is devouring his family?

2. **Inference** Reread page 60. Why does the grandfather tell his grandson that he is stupid and end their conversation?

LOOK AHEAD Read to page 83 to see why a movie leads to children's deaths.

The teacher was surprised when, hearing that they needed a button on the poster to represent the button **industry**, the child tore one off his shirt and offered it to her. She was surprised because she knew that this was probably the only shirt the child had. She didn't know whether he did this to be helpful, to feel like he belonged, or out of love for her. She did feel **the intensity of the child's desire** and this was what surprised her most of all.

....

industry business

the intensity of the child's desire that the child had very strong feelings

The Little Burnt Victims

There were five in the García family. Don Efraín, Doña Chona and their three children: Raulito, Juan, and Maria—seven, six, and five years old, **respectively**. On Sunday evening they arrived from the theater excited over the movie about boxing that they had seen. Don Efraín was the most excited. When they arrived, he brought out the boxing gloves he had bought for the children and then he made them put them on. He even **stripped them down to** their shorts and rubbed a bit of alcohol on their little chests, just like they had seen done in the movie. Doña Chona didn't like for them to box because someone would always end up getting mad and then the wailing would start and last for a long time.

"That's enough, viejo. Why do you make them fight? Remember how Juan's nose always starts to bleed and you know how hard it is to make the bleeding stop. Come on, viejo, let them go to bed."

"Man, vieja!"

....

respectively in that order

stripped them down to made them take off all their clothes except

"I'm not a man."

"Oh, let them fight. Maybe they'll at least learn how to defend themselves."

"But can't you see that we barely have enough room to stand up in this **chicken shack** and there you are running around like we had so much space."

"And what do you think they do when we go to work? I wish they were older so we could take them with us to the fields. They could work or at least sit quietly in the car."

"Yeah, but do you really think so? The older they get, the more **restless** they become. I don't like it at all leaving them here by themselves."

"Maybe one of them will **turn out good with the glove, and then we'll be set** vieja. Just think how much money champions win. Thousands and thousands. I'm gonna see if I can order them a punching bag through the catalog next week, as soon as we get paid."

"Well, true. You never know, right?"

"Right. That's what I'm telling you."

The three children were left to themselves in the house

....

chicken shack tiny place

restless active

turn out good with the glove, and then we'll be set be a great boxer, and then we will not have to worry about money

when they went to work because the owner didn't like children in the fields **doing mischief** and distracting their parents from their work. Once they took them along and kept them in the car, but the day had gotten very hot and suffocating and the children had even gotten sick. From then on they decided to leave them at home instead, although, sure enough, they worried about them all day long. Instead of packing a lunch, they would go home at noon to eat and that way they could check on them to see if they were all right. That following Monday they got up before dawn as usual and left for work. They left the children fast asleep.

"You look real happy, viejo."

"You know why."

"No, it's not just that. You look like you're happier than just because of that."

"It's just that I love my children so much, like you. And on the way I was thinking about how they also like to play with us."

At about ten o'clock that morning, from where they were working in the fields they noticed smoke rising from

....

doing mischief causing trouble

the direction of the farm. Everyone stopped working and ran to their cars. They sped toward the farm. When they arrived they found the García's shack **engulfed in flames**. Only the eldest child was saved. The bodies of the other children were **charred** in the blaze.

"They say that the oldest child made little Juan and María put on the gloves. They were just playing. But then I think he rubbed some alcohol on their chests and who knows what other stuff on their little bodies like they had seen done in the movie. That's how they were playing."

"But how did the fire get started?"

"Well, poor things, the oldest, Raulito, started to fry some eggs while they were playing and somehow or other their little bodies caught on fire, and you can imagine."

"He must have rubbed lots of alcohol on them."

"You know all the junk that piles up in the house, so **cramped for space** and all. I believe the kerosene tank on the stove exploded and . . . that was it. The explosion must have covered them with flames and, of course, the

....

engulfed in flames on fire

charred burned

cramped for space crowded; full of things

shack, too."

"Why, sure."

"And you know what?"

"What?"

"The only thing that didn't get burnt up was the pair of gloves. They say they found the little girl all burnt up and with the gloves on."

"But I wonder why the gloves didn't get burned up?"

"Well, you know how those people can make things so good. Not even fire can destroy them."

"And the Garcías, how are they **getting along**?"

"Well, they're getting over their grief, although I don't believe they'll ever be able to forget it. What else can you do? I tell you, you never know when **your turn's up**. **My heart goes out to them.** But you never know."

"So true."

....

getting along feeling, doing

your turn's up you are going to die

My heart goes out to them. I feel sorry for the Garcías.

It was a beautiful wedding day. Throughout the entire week **prior** the groom and his father had been busy fixing up the yard at the bride's house and setting up a canvas tent where the couple would receive the congratulations of family and friends. For decorations they used the **limbs** of pecan trees and wild flowers and everything was arranged very nicely. Then they smoothed down the ground in front of the tent very neatly. Every little while they sprinkled water on it to pack down the soil. This way the dust wouldn't get stirred up so much once the dancing got started. After they were married in the church the couple strolled down the street followed by a **procession** of godmothers and godfathers and ahead of them a bunch of children running and shouting, "Here come the newlyweds!"

....

prior before the wedding
limbs branches
procession group, line

The Night the Lights Went Out

The night the lights of the town went out some became frightened and others did not. It wasn't storming nor was there any lightning, so some didn't find out until later. Those who were at the dance had found out but those who weren't hadn't . . . until the next day. Those who stayed home just noticed that right after the lights went out the music was no longer heard through the night and they figured that the dance had ended. But they didn't find out anything until the next day.

"That Ramón, he loved his girlfriend a lot. Yes, he loved her a lot. I know so because he was my friend and, well, you know he wasn't one who talked much, but anyway, he would tell me everything. Many times he'd say how much he loved her. They'd been **going together** since last year and they had given each other real pretty rings that they bought at **Kress**. And she loved him, too, but who knows what had happened this summer. They say it was the first time in four months that he had seen her

....

going together dating
Kress the nice store downtown

. . . no one knows, no one really knows . . ."

"Look, I promise you I'm not gonna see anybody
else or flirt with anyone. I promise you. I want to marry
you . . . Look, we can go away together right now if you
want to . . . Well, we'll wait then, until we finish school.
But, look, I promise you I won't **go around with**
anyone else nor flirt with anyone. I promise you. We
can leave right now if you want to. I can support you. **I
know**, I know . . . but they'll **get over it**. Let's go. Will
you go with me?"

"No, it's better to wait, don't you think? It's better if
we do it right. I promise you, too . . . You know that I
love you. Trust me. Dad wants me to finish school. And,
well, I have to do what he says. But that doesn't mean I
don't love you just 'cause I can't go away with you. I do
love you, I love you very much. I won't go around with
anybody else either. I promise you."

"Oh, come on. You know everybody knows. I heard
something else. Somebody told me that she'd been going

....

go around with date
I know I know our parents will not like it
get over it accept it

77

around with some **dude out there** in Minnesota. And that she still kept on writing to Ramón. Kept on lying to him. Some of Ramón's friends told him everything. They were working at the same farm where she was. And then when they saw him out here they told him right off. He was faithful to her but she wasn't. She was going around with some guy from San Antonio. He **was nothing but a show-off and he was always all duded up**. They say he wore orange shoes and real long coats and always had his collar turned up . . . But her, I think she liked to mess around, otherwise she wouldn't have been unfaithful. What was bad was her not breaking up with him. When he found out, Juanita hadn't returned yet from up north and he **took to** drinking a lot. I saw him once when he was drunk and all he would say was that he was hurting. That that was all that women left behind, nothing but pain inside."

"When I get back to Texas I'll take her away with me. I can't go on like this anymore. She'll come with me. She will. She's done me wrong. How I love her. With each swing of this hoe I hear her name. How

....

dude out there other guy while she was

was nothing but a show-off and he was always all duded up
loved to get attention from people and he always looked
good

took to started

come you feel this way when you're in love? I no sooner finish supper and I'm staring at her picture until dark. And at noon, during the lunch hour, too. But the thing is, I don't really remember how she looks. The picture doesn't seem to look like her anymore. Or she doesn't look like the picture. When the others make fun of me, I just go off to the woods. I see the picture but I just don't remember anymore how she looks, even if I see her picture. Maybe it's best to not look at it so much. She promised she'd be faithful. And she is, because her eyes and her smile keep telling me so when I picture her in my mind. Soon it'll be time to return to Texas. Each time I wake to the early **crow** of the roosters I feel like I'm already there and that I'm watching her walk down the street. It won't be long now."

"Well, it's not that I don't love Ramón, but this guy, he's **a real smooth talker** and we just talk, that's all. And all the girls just stare at him. He dresses really fine, too. It's not that I don't love Ramón, but this guy is real nice and his smile, I see it all day long . . . No, I'm not breaking up with Ramón. And, anyway, what's

---

crow sound, singing
a real smooth talker very charming

wrong with just talking? I don't want to **get serious with** this guy, I promised Ramón . . . but he just keeps on following and following me around. I don't want to get serious with him . . . I don't want to lose Ramón, I'm not getting involved with this guy. I just want him around to make the other girls jealous. No, I can't break up with Ramón because I really do love him a lot. It won't be long before we'll see each other again . . . Who said he was talking to Petra? Well, then, why is he always following me around? I'll have you know he even sends me letters every day with Don José's little boy."

". . . I know you're going with someone else but I like talking to you. Since I got here and saw you I want to be with you more and more. Go to the dance Saturday and dance with me all night . . . Love you, Ramiro."

"They say she danced the whole night with Ramiro. I think her friends told her something about it but she just ignored them. This happened about the time when the work season was almost over and at the last dance,

....

get serious with marry; have a serious relationship with

when they were saying good-bye, they promised to see each other back here. I don't think she even remembered Ramón at that moment. But by then Ramón already knew everything. That's why on that day, after not seeing each other in four months, he **threw it all in her face**. I was with him that day, I was with him when he saw her and I remember well that he was so happy to see her that he wasn't mad anymore. But then, after talking to her for a while he started getting mad all over again. They **broke up** right then and there."

"You do whatever you want."

"You can be sure of that."

"You're breaking up with me?"

"Yeah, and if you go to the dance tonight you better not dance with anyone else."

"And why shouldn't I? We're not going around anymore. We broke up. You can't tell me what to do."

"I don't care if we broke up or not. You're gonna **pay for this**. You're gonna do what I say, when I say, and for as long as I say. Nobody makes **a fool out of me**. You're gonna pay for this one, one way or another."

....

threw it all in her face yelled at her
broke up stopped dating
pay for this suffer because of this
a fool out of me me look like a fool

"You can't tell me what to do."

"You're gonna do what I say and if you don't dance with me, you don't dance with anyone. And I mean for the entire dance."

"Well, they say that Juanita asked her parents for permission to leave early for the dance. She went with some of her friends and the **orchestra** hadn't even started playing yet and there they were already at the dance hall, standing by the door so the guys would see them and ask them to dance right away. Juanita had been dancing with only one guy when Ramón got there. He walked in and looked all around for her. He saw her dancing and when the song ended he went over and grabbed her away from the guy. This guy, just a kid, didn't say anything, he just walked away and asked someone else to dance. Anyway, when the music started again Juanita refused to dance with Ramón. They were standing right in the middle of the dance floor and all the other couples were dancing around them. They stood there arguing and then she slapped him, and he yelled something at her and **charged** out of the dance hall. Juanita walked over to a

....

orchestra band, musicians
charged ran

bench and sat down. The song hadn't even ended when all the lights went out. There was a bunch of yelling and screaming and they tried to turn them back on but then they saw that the whole town had **blacked out**."

The workers from the light company found Ramón inside the power plant that was about a block away from the dance hall. They say that his body was **burnt to a crisp** and that he was holding on to one of the **transformers**. That's why all the lights of the town went out. The people at the dance found out almost right away. And the ones who were close to Ramón and Juanita heard him tell her that he was going to kill himself because of her. The people at home didn't find out until the next day, that Sunday morning before and after mass.

"They just loved each other so much, don't you think?"
"No doubt."

....

blacked out no lights
burnt to a crisp badly burnt
transformers wires

BEFORE YOU MOVE ON...

1. **Irony** Why is it ironic that the boxing gloves do not get destroyed in the fire?

2. **Author's Style** Reread page 75. How does the author show that while some people are experiencing tragedy, others are experiencing joy?

LOOK AHEAD Read pages 84–104 to find out how Doña María ends up in jail.

A little before six, just before the spinach pickers would be getting home, there was the **high-pitched signal** of the horn at the water tank, then the sound of fire trucks, and then some moments later the ambulance sirens. By six o'clock some of the workers arrived with the news of how one of the trucks transporting workers had collided with a car and was still burning. When the car hit it, those who were not thrown out of the van **on impact** were trapped. Those who witnessed the crash said that the truck had immediately burst into flames and that they had seen some victims, poor souls, running from the wreckage toward the thicket with their hair **aflame**. They say the Anglo woman driving the car was from a **dry county** and that she'd been at a bar drinking, upset because her husband had left her. There were sixteen dead.

....

high-pitched signal loud sound
on impact when it was hit
aflame on fire
dry county part of the state where liquor is not sold in stores

The Night Before Christmas

Christmas Eve was approaching and the **barrage of** commercials, music, and Christmas cheer over the radio and the blare of announcements over the loud speakers on top of the stationwagon advertising movies at the Teatro Ideal resounded and seemed to **draw it closer**. It was three days before Christmas when Doña María decided to buy something for her children. This was the first time she would buy them toys. Every year she intended to do it but she always ended up **facing up to the fact** that, no, they couldn't afford it. She knew that her husband would be bringing each of the children candies and nuts anyway and, so she would **rationalize** that they didn't need to get them anything else. Nevertheless, every Christmas the children asked for toys. She always appeased them with the same promise. She would tell them to wait until the sixth of January, the day of the Magi, and by the time that day arrived the children had already forgotten all about it. But now she was noticing that each year the children seemed less and less taken with Don Chon's visit on Christmas Eve

....

barrage of large amount of
draw it closer bring Christmas closer
facing up to the fact realizing
rationalize convince herself

when he came **bearing** a sack of oranges and nuts.

"But why doesn't Santa Claus bring us anything?"

"What do you mean? What about the oranges and nuts he brings you?"

"No, that's Don Chon."

"No, I'm talking about what you always find under the sewing machine."

"What, Dad's the one who brings that, don't think we don't know that. Aren't we good like the other kids?"

"Of course, you're good children. Why don't you wait until **the day of the Reyes Magos**. That's when toys and gifts really arrive. In Mexico, it's not Santa Claus who brings gifts, but the Three Wise Men. And they don't come until the sixth of January. That's the real date."

"Yeah, but they always forget. They've never brought us anything, not on Christmas Eve, not on the day of the Three Kings."

"Well, maybe this time they will."

"Yeah, well, I sure hope so."

....

bearing carrying, bringing

the day of the Reyes Magos the Mexican holiday that honors the Three Wise Men

That was why she made up her mind to buy them something. But they didn't have the money to spend on toys. Her husband worked almost eighteen hours a day washing dishes and cooking at a restaurant. He didn't have time to go downtown and buy toys. Besides, they had to save money every week to pay for the trip up north. Now they even charged for children, too, even if they rode standing up the whole way to Iowa. So it cost them a lot to make the trip. In any case, that night when her husband arrived, tired from work, she talked to him about getting something for the children.

"Look, viejo, the children want something for Christmas."

"What about the oranges and nuts I bring them."

"Well, they want toys. They're not content anymore with just fruits and nuts. They're a little older now and **more aware of things**."

"They don't need anything."

"Now, you can't tell me you didn't have toys when you were a kid."

"I used to *make* my own toys, out of clay . . . little

....

more aware of things notice that they do not get any toys

horses and little soldiers . . ."

"Yes, but it's different here. They see so many things
. . . come on, let's go get them something . . . I'll go to
Kress myself."

"You?"

"Yes, me."

"Aren't you afraid to go downtown? You remember
that time in Wilmar, out in Minnesota, how you got lost
downtown. Are you sure you're not afraid?"

"Yes, yes, I remember, but I'll just have to get my
courage up. I've thought about it all day long and **I've
set my mind to it**. I'm sure I won't get lost here.
Look, I go out to the street. From here you can see the
ice house. It's only four blocks away, so Doña Regina
tells me. When I get to the ice house I turn to the right
and go two blocks and there's downtown. Kress is right
there. Then, I come out of Kress, walk back towards the
ice house and turn back on this street, and here I am."

"I guess it really won't be difficult. Yeah. Fine. I'll
leave you some money on top of the table when I go to
work in the morning. But be careful, vieja, there's a lot
of people downtown these days."

....

I've set my mind to it I have decided to go

The fact was that Doña María very rarely left the house. The only time she did was when she visited her father and her sister who lived on the next block. And she only went to church whenever someone died and, occasionally, when there was a wedding. But she went with her husband, so she never took notice of where she was going. And her husband always brought her everything. He was the one who bought the groceries and clothing. **In reality** she was unfamiliar with downtown even though it was only six blocks away. The cemetery was on the other side of downtown and the church was also in that direction. The only time that they passed through downtown was whenever they were on their way to San Antonio or whenever they were returning from up north. And this would usually be during the **wee** hours of the morning or at night. But that day she was determined and she started making preparations.

The next day she got up early as usual, and after seeing her husband and children off, she took the money from the table and began getting ready to go downtown. This didn't take her long.

"My God, I don't know why I'm so fearful. Why,

....

In reality Truthfully
wee early

downtown is only six blocks from here. I just go straight and then after I cross the tracks turn right. Then go two blocks and there's Kress. On the way back, I walk two blocks back and then I turn to the left and keep walking until I'm home again. God willing, there won't be any dogs on the way. And I just pray that the train doesn't come while I'm crossing the tracks and catches me right in the middle . . . I just hope there's no dogs . . . I hope there's no train coming down the tracks."

She walked the distance from the house to the railroad tracks rapidly. She walked down the middle of the street all the way. She was afraid to walk on the sidewalk. She feared she might get bitten by a dog or that someone might grab her. In actuality there was only one dog along the **entire stretch** and most of the people didn't even notice her walking toward downtown. She nevertheless kept walking down the middle of the street and, luckily, not a single car passed by, otherwise she would not have known what to do. Upon arriving at the crossing she **was suddenly struck by** intense fear. She could hear the sound of moving trains and their whistles blowing and this **was unnerving** her. She was

....

entire stretch path that she walked
was suddenly struck by suddenly felt
was unnerving scared

too scared to cross. Each time she mustered enough courage to cross she heard the whistle of the train and, frightened, she retreated and ended up at the same place. Finally, overcoming her fear, she shut her eyes and crossed the tracks. Once she got past the tracks, her fear began to subside. She got to the corner and turned to the right.

The sidewalks were crowded with people and her ears started to fill up with a ringing sound, the kind that, once it started, it wouldn't stop. She didn't recognize any of the people around her. She wanted to turn back but she was caught in the **flow of the crowd which shoved her** onward toward downtown and the sound kept ringing louder and louder in her ears. She became frightened and more and more she was finding herself unable to remember why she was there amidst the crowd of people. She stopped in an alley way between two stores to **regain her composure a bit**. She stood there for a while watching the passing crowd.

"My God, what is happening to me? I'm starting to feel the same way I did in Wilmar. I hope I don't get worse. Let me see . . . the ice house is in that direction—no it's that way. No, my God, what's happening to me?

....

flow of the crowd which shoved her middle of the rushing crowd which pushed her

regain her composure a bit relax; get calm

Let me see . . . I came from over there to here. So it's in that direction. I should have just stayed home. Uh, can you tell me where Kress is, please? . . . Thank you."

She walked to where they had pointed and entered the store. The noise and pushing of the crowd was worse inside. **Her anxiety soared.** All she wanted was to leave the store but she couldn't find the doors anywhere, only stacks and stacks of merchandise and people crowded against one another. She even started hearing voices coming from the merchandise. For a while she stood, **gazing blankly** at what was in front of her. She couldn't even remember the names of the things. Some people stared at her for a few seconds, others just pushed her aside. She remained **in this state** for a while, then she started walking again. She finally made out some toys and put them in her bag. Then she saw a wallet and also put that in her bag. Suddenly she no longer heard the noise of the crowd. She only saw the people moving about—their legs, their arms, their mouths, their eyes. She finally asked where the door, the exit was. They told her and she started in that direction. She pressed through the crowd,

....

Her anxiety soared. She became more scared.
gazing blankly staring
in this state like this

pushing her way until she pushed open the door and exited.

She had been standing on the sidewalk for only a few seconds, trying to figure out where she was, when she felt someone grab her roughly by the arm. She was grabbed so tightly that she gave out a cry.

"Here she is . . . these damn people, always stealing something, stealing. I've been watching you all along. Let's have that bag."

"But . . ."

Then she heard nothing for a long time. All she **saw was the pavement moving swiftly toward her face** and a small pebble that bounced into her eye and was hurting a lot. She felt someone pulling her arms and when they turned her, face up, all she saw were faces far away. Then she saw a security guard with a gun in his holster and she was terrified. In that instant she thought about her children and her eyes filled with tears. She started crying. Then she **lost consciousness of** what was happening around her, only feeling herself drifting in a sea of people, their arms brushing

....

saw was the pavement moving swiftly toward her face felt was someone forcing her to the ground

lost consciousness of fainted and did not know

against her like waves.

"It's a good thing my compadre happened to be there. He's the one who ran to the restaurant to tell me. How do you feel?"

"I think I must be insane, viejo."

"That's why I asked you if you weren't afraid you might get sick like in Wilmar."

"What will become of my children with a mother who's insane? A crazy woman who can't even talk, can't even go downtown."

"Anyway, I went and got the **notary public**. He's the one who went with me to the jail. He explained everything to the official. That you got dizzy and that you get nervous attacks whenever you're in a crowd of people."

"And if they send me to the **insane asylum**? I don't want to leave my children. Please, viejo, don't let them take me, don't let them. I shouldn't have gone downtown."

"Just stay here inside the house and don't leave the yard. There's no need for it anyway. I'll bring you

....

notary public person with the power to defend you

insane asylum hospital for mentally ill people

everything you need. Look, don't cry anymore, don't cry. No, go ahead and cry, it'll make you feel better. I'm gonna talk to the kids and tell them to stop bothering you about Santa Claus. I'm gonna tell them there's no Santa Claus, that way they won't trouble you with that anymore."

"No, viejo, don't be mean. Tell them that if he doesn't bring them anything on Christmas Eve, it's because the Reyes Magos will be bringing them something."

"But . . . well, all right, whatever you say. I suppose it's always best to have hope."

The children, who were hiding behind the door, heard everything, but they didn't quite understand it all. They awaited the day of the Reyes Magos as they did every year. When that day came and went with no arrival of gifts, they didn't ask for explanations.

Before people left for up north the priest would bless their cars and trucks at five dollars each. One time he made enough money to take a trip to Barcelona, in Spain, to visit his parents and friends. He brought back words of gratitude from his family and some postcards of a very modern church. These he placed by the entrance of the church for the people to see, that they might desire a church such as that one. It wasn't long before words began to appear on the cards, then crosses, lines, and **con safos symbols**, just as had happened to the new church **pews**. The priest was never able to understand the sacrilege.

....

con safos symbols warnings
pews benches

The Portrait

As soon as the people returned from up north the portrait salesmen began arriving from San Antonio. They would come to **rake in**. They knew that the workers had money and that was why, as Dad used to say, they would **flock** in. They carried suitcases packed with samples and always wore white shirts and ties. That way they looked more important and the people believed everything they would tell them and invite them into their homes without giving it much thought. I think that down deep they even longed for their children to one day be like them. In any event, they would arrive and make their way down the dusty streets, going house to house carrying suitcases full of samples.

I remember once I was at the house of one of my father's friends when one of these salesmen arrived. I also remember that that particular one seemed a little frightened and timid. Don Mateo asked him to come in because he wanted to do business.

....

rake in make money
flock rush, come

"Good afternoon, traveler. I would like to tell you about something new that we're offering this year."

"Well, let's see, let's see . . ."

"Well, sir, see, you give us a picture, any picture you may have, and we will not only **enlarge it** for you but we'll also set it in a wooden frame like this one and with **inlays**, like this—three dimensional, as they say."

"And what for?"

"So that it will look real. That way . . . look, let me show you . . . see? Doesn't he look real, like he's alive?"

"Man, he sure does. Look, vieja. This looks great. Well, you know, we wanted to send some pictures to be enlarged . . . but now, this must cost a lot, right?"

"No, I'll tell you, it costs about the same. Of course, it takes more time."

"Well, tell me, how much?"

"For as little as thirty dollars we'll deliver it to you done with inlays just like this, one this size."

"Boy, that's expensive! Didn't you say it didn't cost a lot more? **Do you take installments?**"

"Well, I'll tell you, we have a new manager and he wants everything in cash. It's very fine work. We'll make

....

enlarge it make it bigger

inlays extra layers of material; a design

Do you take installments? Can I pay for it a little at a time?

it look like real. Done like that, with inlays . . . take a look. What do you think? Some fine work, wouldn't you say? We can have it all finished for you in a month. You just tell us what color you want the clothes to be and we'll come by with it all finished one day **when you least expect**, framed and all. Yes, sir, a month at the longest. But like I say, this man who's the new manager, he wants the full payment in cash. He's very demanding, even with us."

"Yes, but it's much too expensive."

"Well, yes. But the thing is, this is very fine work. You can't say you've ever seen portraits done like this, with wood inlays."

"No, well, that's true. What do you think, vieja?"

"Well, I like it a lot. Why don't we order one? And if it turns out good . . . my Chuy . . . may he rest in peace. It's the only picture we have of him. We took it right before he left for Korea. Poor m'ijo, we never saw him again. See . . . this is his picture. Do you think you can make it like that, make it look like he's alive?"

"Sure, we can. You know, we've done a lot of them in soldier's uniforms and shaped it, like you see in this

....

when you least expect and surprise you

sample, with inlays. Why, it's more than just a portrait. Sure. You just tell me what size you want and whether you want a round or square frame. **How should I write it down?**"

"What do you say, vieja, should we have it done like this one?"

"Well, I've already told you what I think. I would like to have m'ijo's picture fixed up like that and in color."

"All right, go ahead and write it down. But you take good care of that picture for us because it's the only one we have of our son grown up. He was going to send us one all dressed up in uniform with the American and Mexican flags crossed over his head, but he no sooner got there when a letter arrived telling us that he was **lost in action**. So you take good care of it."

"Don't you worry. We're responsible people. And we understand the sacrifices that you people make. Don't worry. And you just wait and see. When we bring it to you you'll see how pretty it's gonna look. What do you say, should we make the uniform navy blue?"

"But he's not wearing a uniform in that picture."

....

How should I write it down? What would you like to order?

lost in action killed in the war

"No, but that's just a matter of fixing it up with some wood fiber overlays. Look at these. This one, he didn't have a uniform on but we put one on him. So what do you say? Should we make it navy blue?"

"All right."

"Don't you worry about the picture."

And that was how they spent the entire day going house to house, street by street, their suitcases stuffed with pictures. **As it turned out**, a whole lot of people had ordered enlargements of that kind.

"They should be delivering those portraits soon, don't you think?"

"I think so, it's delicate work and takes more time. That's some fine work those people do. Did you see how real those pictures looked?"

"Yeah, sure. They do some fine work. You can't deny that. But it's already been over a month since they passed by here."

"Yes, but from here they went on through all the towns picking up pictures . . . all the way to San Antonio

....

As it turned out By the end of the day

for sure. So it'll probably take a little longer."

"That's true, that's true."

And two more weeks had passed by the time they made the discovery. Some very heavy rains had come and some children who were playing in one of the tunnels leading to the dump found a sack full of pictures, all worm-eaten and soaking wet. The only reason they could tell that these were pictures was because there were a lot of them and most of them the same size and with faces that could just barely be made out. **Everybody caught on right away.** Don Mateo was so angry that he took off to San Antonio to find the so and so who had **swindled them**.

"Well, you know, I stayed at Esteban's house. And every day I went with him to the market to sell produce. I helped him with everything. I had faith that I would run into that **son of a gun** some day soon. Then, after I'd been there for a few days, I started going out to the different barrios and I found out a lot that way. It wasn't so much the money that upset me. It was my poor vieja, crying and all because we'd lost the only picture we

....

Everybody caught on right away. Everybody realized the salesmen had fooled them.

swindled them tricked them and taken their money

son of a gun thief

had of Chuy. We found it in the sack with all the other pictures but it was already ruined, you know."

"I see, but tell me, how did you find him?"

"Well, you see, **to make a long story short**, he came by the stand at the market one day. He stood right in front of us and bought some vegetables. It was like he was trying to remember who I was. Of course, I recognized him right off. Because when you're angry enough, you **don't forget a face**. I just grabbed him right then and there. Poor guy couldn't even talk. He was all scared. And I told him that I wanted that portrait of my son and that I wanted it three dimensional and that he'd best get it for me or I'd let him have it. And I went with him to where he lived. And I put him to work right then and there. The poor guy didn't know where to begin. He had to **do it all from memory**."

"And how did he do it?"

"I don't know. I suppose if you're scared enough, you're capable of doing anything. Three days later he brought me the portrait all finished, just like you see it there on that table by the Virgin Mary. Now tell me, how do you like the way my boy looks?"

....

to make a long story short to quickly tell you

don't forget a face remember the person that hurt you

do it all from memory recreate the picture without looking at the photo

"Well, to be honest, I don't remember too well how Chuy looked. But he was beginning to look more and more like you, isn't that so?"

"Yes, I would say so. That's what everybody tells me now. That **Chuy's a chip off the old block** and that he was already looking like me. There's the portrait. Like they say, one and the same."

....

Chuy's a chip off the old block Chuy was similar to me

BEFORE YOU MOVE ON...

1. **Conclusions** Why is it so important to Doña María that her children get presents?

2. **Cause and Effect** How and why do the portrait salespeople take advantage of the migrant workers?

LOOK AHEAD The migrant workers want to change their lives. Read pages 105–126 to find out why.

"They let Figueroa out. He's been out a week."

"Yeah, but he's not well. There in **the pen**, if they don't like someone, they'll give them **injections** so they'll die."

"Damn right. Who do you think turned him in?"

"Probably some gringo who couldn't stand seeing him in town with that white girl he brought back with him from Wisconsin. And no one to defend him. They say the little gringa was seventeen and it's against the law."

"I'll bet you he won't last a year."

"Well, they say he has a very strange disease."

....

the pen jail
injections poison

When We Arrive

At about four o'clock in the morning the truck broke down. All night they stood **hypnotized** by the high-pitched **whir** of the tires turning against the pavement. When the truck stopped they awakened. The silence alone told them something was wrong. All along the way the truck had been overheating and then when they stopped and checked the motor they saw that it had practically burned up. It just wouldn't go anymore. They would have to wait there until daybreak and then ask for a **lift** to the next town. Inside the trailer the people awakened and then **struck up** several conversations. Then in the darkness their eyes had gradually begun to close and all became so silent that all that could be heard was the chirping of the crickets. Some were sleeping, others were thinking.

"Good thing the truck stopped here. My stomach's been hurting a lot for some time but I would've had to wake up a lot of people to get to the window and ask them to stop. But you still can't hardly see anything.

....

hypnotized fascinated
whir noise
lift ride
struck up began

Well, I'm getting off, see if I can find a field or a ditch. Must've been that chile I ate, it was so hot but I hated to let it go to waste. I hope my vieja is doing all right in there, carrying the baby and all."

"This driver that we have this year is a good one. He keeps on going. He doesn't stop for anything. Just **gases up and let's go**. We've been on the road over twenty-four hours. We should be close to Des Moines. Sure wish I could sit down for just a little while at least. I'd get out and lie down on the side of the road but there's no telling if there's snakes or some other kind of animal. Just before I fell asleep on my feet it felt like my knees were going to **buckle**. But I guess your body gets used to it right away 'cause it doesn't seem so hard anymore. But the kids must feel real tired standing like this all the way and with nothing to hold on to. Us grownups can at least hold on to this center bar that supports the canvas. And to think we're not as crowded as other times. I think there must be forty of us at the most. I remember that one time I traveled with that bunch of wetbacks, there were more than sixty of us. We couldn't even smoke."

....

gases up and let's go stops to get gas for the truck and then keeps going

buckle bend and let me fall

"What a stupid woman! How could she be so dumb as to throw that diaper out the front of the truck. It came sliding along the canvas and good thing I had glasses on or I would even have gotten the crap in my eyes! What a stupid woman! How could she do that? She should've known that crap would be blown towards all of us standing up back here. Why the hell couldn't she just wait until we got to a gas station and dump the crap there!"

"**El Negrito** just stood there in disbelief when I ordered the fifty-four hamburgers. At two in the morning. And since I walked into the restaurant alone and I'm sure he didn't see the truck pull up loaded with people. **His eyes just popped wide open** . . . 'at two o'clock in the morning, hamburgers? Fifty-four of them? Man, you must **eat one hell of** a lot.' It's that the people hadn't eaten and the driver asked for just one of us to get out and order for everyone. El Negrito was astounded. He couldn't believe what I ordered, that I wanted fifty-four hamburgers. At two o'clock in the morning you can eat that many hamburgers very easily, especially when you're starving."

....

El Negrito The black cashier (in Spanish)
His eyes just popped wide open He was shocked
eat one hell of really eat

"This is the last year I come out here. As soon as we get to the farm I'm getting the hell out. I'll go look for a job in Minneapolis. I'll be damned if I go back to Texas. Out here you can at least make a living at a decent job. I'll look for my uncle, see if he can find me a job at the hotel where he works **as a bellboy**. Who knows, maybe they'll **give me a break** there or at some other hotel. And then the gringas, that's just a matter of finding them."

"If things go well this year, maybe we'll buy us a car so we won't have to travel this way, **like cattle**. The girls are pretty big now and I know they feel embarrassed. Sometimes they have some good buys at the gas stations out there. I'll talk to my compadre, he knows some of the car salesmen. I'll get one I like, even if it's old. I'm tired of coming out here in a truck like this. My compadre drove back a good little car last year. If we do well with the onion crop, I'll buy **me one that's at least half-way decent**. I'll teach my boy how to drive and he can take it all the way to Texas. As long as he

....

as a bellboy carrying luggage
give me a break give me a chance to work
like cattle all crowded together with no room to sit
me one that's at least half-way decent a car

doesn't get lost like my nephew. They didn't stop to ask for directions and ended up in New Mexico instead of Texas. Or I'll get Mundo to drive it and I won't charge him for gas. I'll see if he wants to."

"With the money Mr. Thompson loaned me we have enough to buy food for at least two months. By then we should have the money from the beet crop. Just hope we don't **get too much in debt**. He loaned me two-hundred dollars but by the time you pay for the trip practically half of it is gone, and now that they've started charging me half-fare for the children . . . And then when we return, I have to pay him back double. Four-hundred dollars. That's too much interest, but what can you do? When you need it, you need it. Some people have told me to report him because that's way too much interest but now he's even got the **deed to the** house. I'm just hoping that things go okay for us with the beet crop or else **we'll be left to the wind, homeless**. We have to save enough to pay him back the four hundred. And then we'll see if we have something left. And these kids, they need to start going to school. I don't know. I

....

get too much in debt owe people too much money

deed to the papers that show he is the owner of our

we'll be left to the wind, homeless he will own our house
and we will be homeless

hope it goes okay for us, if not I don't know how we're going to do it. I just pray to God that there's work."

"Damn life, this damn life! This damn life for being **pendejo**! pendejo! pendejo! We're nothing but a bunch of stupid asses! To hell with this damn life! This is the last time I go through this, standing up all the way like an animal. As soon as we get there I'm headed for Minneapolis. Somehow I'll find me something to do where I don't have to work like a mule. Damn life! One of these days they'll pay for this."

"Poor viejo. He must be real tired now, standing up the whole trip. I saw him **nodding off** a little while ago. And with no way to help him, what with these two in my arms. How I wish we were there already so we could lie down, even if it's on the hard floor. These children are nothing but trouble. I hope I'll be able to help him out in the fields, but I'm afraid that this year, what with these kids, I won't be able to do anything. I have to breastfeed them every little while and then they're still so little. If only they were just a bit older. I'm still going

....

pendejo stupid (in Spanish)
nodding off falling asleep

to try my best to help him out. At least **along his row** so he won't feel so overworked. Even if it's just for short whiles. My poor viejo . . . the children are still so little and already he wishes they could start school. I just hope I'll be able to help him. God willing, I'll be able to help him."

"**What a great view of the stars** from here! It looks like they're coming down and touching the **tarp** of the truck. It's almost like there aren't any people inside. There's hardly any traffic at this hour. Every now and then a trailer passes by. The silence of the morning twilight makes everything look like it's made of **satin**. And now, what do I wipe myself with? Why couldn't it always be early dawn like this? We're going to be here till midday for sure. By the time they find help in the town and then by the time they fix the motor . . . If only it could stay like early dawn, then nobody would complain. I'm going to keep my eyes on the stars till the last one disappears. I wonder how many more people are watching the same star? And how many more might there be wondering how many are looking at the same

---

along his row with the crops that he is assigned to
What a great view of the stars You can see the stars
tarp covering
satin shiny cloth

star? It's so silent it looks like it's the stars the crickets are calling to."

"Damn truck. It's nothing but trouble. When we get there everybody will just have to look out for themselves. All I'm doing is dropping them off with the growers and I'm getting the hell out. Besides, **we don't have a contract**. They'll find themselves somebody to take them back to Texas. Somebody's bound to come by and pick them up. You can't make money off beets anymore. My best bet is to head back to Texas just as soon as I drop these people off and then see how things go hauling watermelons. The melon season's almost here. All I need now is for there not to be anyone in this damn town who can fix the truck. What the hell will I do then? So long as the cops don't come by and start **hassling** me about moving the truck from here. Boy, that town had to be the worst. We didn't even stop and still the cop caught up with us just to tell us that he didn't want us staying there. I guess he just wanted to show off in front of the town people. But we didn't even stop in their damn town. When we get there, as soon as I drop them

....

we don't have a contract we have not signed an agreement that forces us to drive them

hassling bothering

off, I'll turn back. **Each one to fend for himself.**"

"When we get there I'm gonna see about getting a good bed for my vieja. Her kidneys are really bothering her a lot nowadays. Just hope we don't end up in a chicken coop like last year, with that cement floor. Even though you cover it with straw, once the cold season sets in you just can't stand it. That was why my **rheumatism** got so bad, I'm sure of that."

"When we arrive, when we arrive, the real truth is that I'm tired of arriving. Arriving and leaving, it's the same thing because we no sooner arrive and . . . the real truth of the matter . . . I'm tired of arriving. I really should say when we don't arrive because that's the real truth. We never arrive."

"When we arrive, when we arrive . . ."

Little by little the crickets ceased their chirping. It seemed as though they were becoming tired and the dawn

....

Each one to fend for himself. Every person in the truck will have to protect and take care of himself.

rheumatism muscle disease; body pains

gradually **affirmed the presence of objects**, ever so carefully and very slowly, so that no one would take notice of what was happening. And the people were becoming people. They began getting out of the trailer and they **huddled around and commenced** to talk about what they would do when they arrived.

....

affirmed the presence of objects made the objects around them visible

huddled around and commenced gathered together and began

Bartolo passed through town every December when he knew that most of the people had returned from work up north. He always came by selling his poems. By the end of the first day, they were almost **sold out** because the names of the people of the town appeared in the poems. And when he read them aloud it was something emotional and serious. I recall that one time he told the people to read the poems out loud because **the spoken word was the seed of love in the darkness**.

....

sold out all sold

the spoken word was the seed of love in the darkness the words made people happy

Under the House

The fleas made him move. He was under a house. He had been there for several hours, or so it seemed to him, hiding. That morning on his way to school he felt the urge not to go. He thought of how the teacher would **spank him for sure** because he didn't know the words. Then he thought of crawling under the house but not just because of that. He felt like hiding, too, but he didn't know where nor for how long, so he just went ahead and hid there. At first the fleas didn't bother him and he felt very comfortable in the dark. Although he was sure there were spiders, he had crawled in unafraid and there he remained. From where he was all he could make out was a white strip of daylight, about a foot high, lining the house all around. He was lying face down and whenever he moved he could feel his back brush against the floor of the house. This even **gave him a feeling of security**. But once the fleas started biting him he had to move constantly. And he started to worry that the people who lived there might find out that he was there and make him get out. But he had to keep moving constantly.

....

spank him for sure hit him; punish him
gave him a feeling of security made him feel safe

*I wonder how long I've been here now. The kids came out of the house to play some time ago. It seems I've been here for a good while. As long as they don't look under the house 'cause they'll see me for sure, and then what? The children look funny, all I can see are their legs running. It's not bad here. I could come here every day. I think that must be what the others do when they **play hooky**. No one to bother me here. I can think in peace.*

He had even forgotten all about the fleas and even that he was under the house. He could think very clearly in the dark. He didn't need to close his eyes. He thought about his father for a while, about how he used to tell him stories at night about witches and how he would make them fall from the sky by praying and tying the seven knots.

*When I'd be coming back from work, at that time we had our own land with **irrigation**, in the early morning twilight, I'd always see these **globes** of light, like fireballs, bouncing off the telephone lines. They would come from the direction of Morelos, they say that's where they originate. One time I nearly made one fall down. Don Remigio taught me how to say the seven*

....

play hooky *do not go to school*
irrigation *pipes that watered our crops*
globes *circles*

prayers that go with the seven knots. All you have to do is
start praying when you see those balls of fire. After each prayer
you tie a knot. This one time I got to the seventh prayer but
you know I wasn't able to tie that last knot, but the witch fell
anyway, practically landing at my feet, and then she got up . . .
The boy was so young and children don't understand too much
at that age. And he couldn't hold out. They're not going to do
*anything to the boss, he's got **too much pull**. Can you imagine*
what they'd do if one of us killed one of their kids? They say
that one day the boy's father took a rifle and went looking for
him because he wanted to pay him back but he didn't find him
. . . The woman would almost always start crying when she
entered the church, and then she'd start praying. But before she
was even aware of it, she would start talking in a loud voice.
Then she'd start yelling, like she was having some kind of attack
. . . I think Doña Cuquita is still living. I haven't seen her in
a long time. She used to be very careful whenever we went to
the dump. Now her I really loved. And since I never knew my
grandparents. I think even Dad loved her like a grandmother
because he, too, never knew his grandparents. What I liked best
was for her to embrace me and tell me, "You're smarter than
***an eagle and more watchful than the moon"** . . . Get out*

---

too much pull *a lot of power*

an eagle and more watchful than the moon *a bird and aware of everything around you*

of there! Get away from that damn window! Go away! Go away . . . You know, you can't come home with me anymore. Look, I don't mind playing with you but some old ladies told mama that Mexicans steal and now mama says not to bring you home anymore. You have to turn back. But we can still play at school. I'll choose you and you choose me . . . What can I tell you! I know what I'm telling you, I'm saying that we can't get **any more screwed** than we already are. I know why I'm telling you. If there's another war, we won't be the ones to suffer. Don't be a damn fool. The ones who will pay for it are the ones on top, the ones who have something. Us, we're already screwed. If there's another war, hell, things might even get better for us . . . Why don't you eat sweet bread anymore? You don't like it, anymore? . . . Well, I tell you, I even went downtown and bought me a new hammer so I could be ready for when they'd come to teach us. They say that the minister, when he found out, he went straight home, took a hatchet and broke all the furniture to pieces and then he took everything outside and set it on fire. He stood there and watched everything burn to ashes . . . I don't think my viejo is going to be able to work out in the sun anymore. The boss didn't say a thing when we told him that he had gotten sick from the heat. He just shook his head.

....

any more screwed *any poorer*

*What worried him the most was that it was raining too much and the crop was getting ruined. That was the only thing he was sad about. He wasn't even sad when they had to operate on his wife because she had cancer, much less when we told him about my viejo . . . These sonofabitches are gonna cut your hair. I'll see to that, if I have to **bust their noses** . . . There is no devil, there isn't. The only devil is Don Rayos when he dresses up with horns and with the cape to go to the shepherds' play . . . Damn fool! Why don't you pay attention to what you're doing? You almost crashed with that truck! Didn't you see it? Are you blind, or what? . . . Why did the teacher cry when they came for him? Ever since he was put in her class she always just kept looking at him. And she was so young, she wasn't like the ones in Texas, little old ladies holding a paddle in their hands making sure you didn't lose your place in the book. And if you did, pow! They'd just bend you over . . . You think that was how they were burned? It's just hard to believe. But so fast? It's that fire spreads fast and once your clothes catch on fire, that's it. You remember that family that died in that fire around Christmas time? They fell asleep, never to wake up again. And then the firemen crying as they removed the bodies, the grease from the children's little burned up bodies dripping all over their boots*

....

bust their noses *hit them in their faces*

*. . . Free citizens, this is a day of magnificent and **profound** importance. It was in the year eighteen-hundred and seventy-two that Napoleon's troops suffered a defeat against Mexican soldiers who fought so **valiantly**—that was how I would begin my **discourse**. I always used the words "free citizens" when I was young, son, but now ever since I had the attack I can't remember too well anymore what I would say to the people. Then came the Revolution and in the end we lost. Villa made out well but I had to come out here. No one here knows what I went through. Sometimes I want to remember but, truth is, I'm not able to anymore. All my thoughts become hazy. Now, tell me, what is it that you most desire at this moment of your life? At this very moment . . . Yesterday we collected fifty pounds of copper in all. Enrique found a magnet and that makes it much easier to find the iron buried under so much junk that people throw away. Sometimes we do well but usually it's a waste of time. But at least enough to buy something to eat. And tell me, what's the price of tin these days? Why don't you all come with us next time we go? . . . The cold weather is **setting in**. I'll bet you that tomorrow morning the ground will be all covered with frost. And notice how often the cranes fly by . . . There's going to be a wedding Sunday. For sure they'll serve us cabrito in mole sauce,*

---

profound *great*
valiantly *courageously*
discourse *talk, speech*
setting in *beginning*

with rice, and then the dance, and the groom, anxious for night to arrive . . . I tell you, comadre . . . we got so frightened last night when the lights went out. We were there playing with the children when all of a sudden it was pitch dark. And we didn't even have one candle. But that wasn't why we got frightened. That **knucklehead**, Juan, was eating an orange and we don't know how but he got a seed in his nose and we couldn't get it out in the dark. And he was just crying and crying. And your compadre, lighting match after match. I wonder what happened. Why, all the lights of the town went out . . . They found Doña Amada's son in a ditch and Don Tiburcio's son inside the trailer. I think they're going to sue Don Jesús for transporting people in a closed van. They say that when they tried to stretch out his body, because they found him all curled up in a corner, when they tried to stretch him out to put him in the **hearse**, one of his legs fell off . . . Those people who sell those portraits don't come around here anymore. Don Mateo gave them a good scare . . . Mom nearly lost her mind. She always started crying whenever she talked with anyone about what happened to her downtown.

I would like to see all of the people together. And then, if

....

knucklehead *stupid person*
hearse *funeral car*

*I had great big arms, I could **embrace** them all. I wish I could talk to all of them again, but all of them together. But that, only in a dream. I like it right here because I can think about anything I please. Only by being alone can you bring everybody together. That's what I needed to do, hide, so that I could come to understand a lot of things. From now on, all I have to do is to come here, in the dark, and think about them. And I have so much to think about and I'm missing so many years. I think today what I wanted to do was recall this past year. And that's just one year. I'll have to come here to recall all of the other years.*

He became aware of the present when he heard one of the children yelling and at the same time felt **a blow to** his leg. They were throwing rocks at him under the house.

"**Mami**, mami, there's a man under the house! Mami, mami, mami, hurry, come here, there's a man here, there's a man here!"

"Where? Where? Ah! . . . Let me get some boards and you run and get Doña Luz's dog."

....

embrace *hug*
a blow to something hit
Mami Mom (in Spanish)

And he saw **countless** faces and eyes looking at him. Then it grew darker under the house. The children kept throwing rocks at him and the dog kept barking while the woman was trying to poke him with some boards.

"Who could it be?"

He had to come out. Everyone was surprised that it was him. He didn't say anything to them, just walked away. And then he heard the woman say:

"That poor family. First the mother and now him. He must be losing his mind. He's losing track of the years."

Smiling, he walked down the **chuckhole-ridden** street leading to his house. He immediately felt happy because, as he thought over what the woman had said, he realized that in reality he hadn't lost anything. He had made a discovery. To discover and rediscover and **piece** things together. This to this, that to that, all with all. That was it. That was everything. He was thrilled. When he got home he went straight to the tree that was in the yard. He climbed it. He saw a palm tree on the horizon. He imagined someone

....

countless many
chuckhole-ridden bumpy
piece put

perched on top, gazing across at him. He even raised one arm and waved it back and forth so that the other could see that he knew he was there.

BEFORE YOU MOVE ON...

1. **Paraphrase** On page 114, the character says that people like him "never arrive." What does he mean?

2. **Character's Motive** Reread page 124. Why does the boy want to embrace everybody in his community?